The Diary
of
Mattie Grey

*Some of the images used in this volume have been adapted from Clipart.
com by subscription, copyright 2008.*

Second, revised edition.

Library of Congress Cataloging-in-Publication Data
Huffman, Joy.
The Diary of Mattie Grey
ISBN 0985273267
ISBN 13 9780985273262
April 2012

Design by PenworthyLLC, Radford, Virginia
Cover art by Cathy Hewes Ceritano

Printed in the United States.

My Diary is the process of memory and imagination.
The entries, from an early age to the present, are like
reading from an account written over many years,
the difference being that while paper will yellow and
crumble and the ink fade, the mind with its power
of memory is indelible

Foreword

This book was a pleasure to read: almost poetic prose (which was not a surprise to me), charm, vivid imagery, and tender relationships among generous creatures. And the humor is subtle and natural. Obviously here is the accumulated wisdom of a long, good and very real life. Few modern writers know so much about the growing, the seasonal changes, the little beauties of the day and night hours, and the small, regular comforts of a quiet life.

The rich descriptions, aphorisms, and bits of sentiment and awe that are written in, those are the essence, those are the touches that make this a really special book.

James Alexander Thom
author of, among others, *Follow the River, Children of the First Man, The Red Heart* and *Panther in the Sky*.

Prologue

I, aka Mattie Grey, a mouse that made tracks, was born and reared in Craig County, Virginia, in a time when children were allowed that magic time between birth and young adulthood to work and play and learn. Both of my parents worked very hard to make a living. Being farm people, though, they had a certain assurance that by their efforts the necessities of life would be met. I picked up on this early in life, and as I ran with a little bucket toward the spring, I picked the flowers, spilled most of the water and was touched by everything the seasons brought. With the call of whippoorwills as night came on, I drifted off to sleep knowing my mother was near and could fix whatever was wrong.

I have now lived through my early years, my middle years, and I suspect that I am living in my last years. Being at this stage of life, I feel qualified to pass on a bit of information I have learned by trial and error; to be truthful – many trials and even more errors. It is from this heritage that the idea of Mattie Grey was conceived.

Communication being what it is, words fail to convey the depth of emotion that strikes the core, the cords of the fabric of our being. *The Diary of Mattie Grey* is such an attempt, for we all have a need to be heard.

Many times when I think of my childhood, all of life pales when compared to it. The beauty and mystery of the natural world crowded in upon my every sense -- the ability of the earth to support and sustain life day by day and the steady, sure coming of the night, when we are renewed and sustained to live yet another day by the connection of a single breath.

From these early days, I would live many years before my feelings would become thoughts and finally form into words I could utter. It was a time when travel and the splendor of resort living brought many people to the great inns and hotels to experience rural living. Many of my distant relatives worked at these places, and I am sure that long before I could reason, the influence of such splendor was impressed upon my mind.

It was during those years that I would learn lessons that would serve me all the days of my life. These were lessons of generosity and compassion, the commodities that come from a storehouse that can never be exhausted.

As I interacted with everything that had life, I would come to realize that within my grasp, *in my own hands*, was the raw material of life. The great vistas of beauty are never an end in themselves, but only stages in greater blessings. I have said elsewhere, "The plum is a white blossom before it is purple."

In the economy of the earth, all things are numbered by the million, the billion and the trillion, from the stars we see at night, through our knowledge of seed, to the imprint of the individual, the multitudes of people who are alive, plus all who have lived and those not yet born. This design is no less real, no less evident, even though we do not understand it.

Among the many lessons I learned is that labor always pays a fair wage, so I worked at whatever I was able to. There were many opportunities to help. Where we lived, there was no water on the place, so one of my first jobs was carrying water in a syrup bucket that held one half-gallon.

Instruction is a shallow thing compared to the experience I gained from watching my parents work each day to secure the necessities we needed to survive. I remember their efforts and talents in making the most of life day by day. In addition to working hard to make ends meet, they each had pleasurable pursuits.

My daddy loved to fox hunt, and he bred and raised hunting hounds for this sport. I have great memories of the soft, squirming puppies, as I pulled them through the fence. I can remember to this day how they felt and smelled. My mother grew many flowers, and at one time the flowers and I were about the same height. This memory is filled with color, form and perfume—the gifts of beauty that decorate all the days of our lives. Bright, happy days and bright, happy memories!

The farm animals had to be nurtured and cared for, as each of them played an important role in the survival of all. I gathered eggs, carried in wood to fill the wood box behind the kitchen stove, and picked berries. However, the one job I remember the most is the love and care I gave to a cow named Elsie.

Elsie was a beautiful, dependable, brindled Jersey cow, whose milk was as plentiful and sweet as the summer grass she grazed on. Her color was mixed by nature's richest hues: the brown and gold and russet tints all as rich as the cream that rose above her milk. She had medium, well-shaped horns and expressive eyes that were thickly lashed.

Out of her eyes flashed the light of life that I was so bound to. It was a light that gave me a merry heart and a willingness to nurture and give back to the cow. She had a jolly temperament, and many times would jump and kick up her hooves. That magic beam of life is still within reach every time I think of Elsie.

Elsie lived in a barn that was a wonderful, big building that held the very scents of summer: the perfume of harvested hay and straw, with their essence of clover and other green grasses that were now brown and dried for the winter. I loved the barn and played there throughout all the seasons. I would often climb to the loft window and look out over my whole world and dream of the unspeakable glories that existed all around me. My childhood was a time to dream, both day and night. I often thought, "This is my world."

In the fall, I would climb between the strands of fence wire that enclosed the orchard and pick up apples that lay thick on the ground for Elsie to eat. I remember the tub that held the apples. It was a galvanized one-half-bushel container. I would linger awhile beside the feedbox and listen to the sound of the apples being crunched as the juice ran out of Elsie's mouth.

During the summer, the cattle would band together and roam in many directions to find the choice grass. It was my job to find Elsie around milking time and drive her home. Many times some of the neighbors would call out a greeting and say, "I saw the cattle around Simpson's hill," or, maybe, "The cows are down at the pump house." Sometimes I would find them at a place we called the Persimmon Pond, resting and peacefully chewing their cud after a long day of grazing.

During this time, I cleaned the stable, threw hay down from the loft for Elsie to munch on at night, and put out clean, bright, yellow straw in a corner of the barn for her to sleep on. A feed barrel held daisy middlings that Elsie ate in the winter, and always a little at milking time. In time, I learned to milk, then strain and take care of the rich pail of milk that Elsie gave in exchange for her care and keep. The cow and I shared in the rich farm life that was green and peaceful in the summer and warm and safe in the wintertime.

Over time, I grew more capable and had other jobs that I was paid to do. Some of the first ones were caring for neighborhood children and selling the berries I picked from the broad fields and banks where the berry-briars grew thick. During this time, I felt very rich, for the berries sold for 25 cents a gallon. Also, mothers soon learned their children would be safe in my care. Most of the time, I just played with them, for in reality I was one of them. The babies were like dolls to me. The only difference was I had experience in responsibility. I had been responsible for a cow, and I had passed the test.

At an early age, I felt the awe and wonder of life, and I could not tell if the song was coming from my heart or from some source outside myself. I would learn in time from life that happiness has its own song, when the highest moments are stamped into the present to last forever.

The gift of memory enables us to keep the very best, and so I remember the early years and the relationship I had with a cow named Elsie.

As the years have passed, Mattie and I have grown very close – in fact, so close that we are now much the same person. Before Mattie came, the place was not only empty, but drab, and not nearly so happy a place as it is today. For, you see, as I invented the mouse, I have become much like her, and this is the most important thing I can say about *The Diary of Mattie Grey*. In all the bountiful seasons I have looked through the knothole, and now in the twilight years, I see even more clearly the act of life unfolding.

This diary is a collection of thoughts and observations from childhood that continued to grow into adulthood and now into old age: that the earth is steady, nature is determined, time hurries and human nature may need glasses. Still, as we age, we finally see more clearly and come to know that life is the only thing that matters. As Mattie would say, entertain the idea often that it is the mind that makes us happy or sad, rich or poor, well or ill, welcome or unwelcome and wise or otherwise.

With Love and Gratitude
Joy Huffman (a Mouse named Mattie)
Pembroke, VA
August 2012

A Time to Be Born

The birth rate has exploded all over the Earth until it can hardly turn. Birth is our first experience with pain, and the shadow of Death follows us all the days of our life. But the days in between glisten with hope that makes it all worthwhile, and the drama of Night gets the attention of even a mouse.

One summer day, when the yard surrounding the nest was filled with chickens singing and scratching for a living and the land was Emerald green with the grass of Summer, I was born into a family that looked to the Meadow for a living also. Many generations have since come and gone, and we all have put up with many hardships, dangers and pollution. There are so many of us now in the Meadow we can hardly support ourselves, and great danger is on every side as we each struggle to get a fair share of the common wealth. With numbers come much pollution of the water, food and even the air we breathe. Our daily habits make a deeper rut in our beings than our tracks make in the ground.

In spite of the hardships, the Meadow has great Beauty that fills each day from the rising of the sun until the magnificence of its setting. Then the Night takes up the burden of trying to get our attention, and above all else the Meadow is home.

I lived in this worldly condition for many years, trying to see the beauty of life in spite of all that was hovering near. We all ran great circles never gaining any ground. I always had an uneasy feeling, looking over my shoulder and hoping something would change.

One day change did come and from the strangest direction, for on that day I took another path and that has made all the difference. My tracks took me far beyond the Meadow. I found myself looking into the inside of a wonderful little house. The house looked like a castle to me.

As I looked farther, I saw a garden. For some time I stood there trying to imagine my life in such a place and my heart beat faster and faster, until at last I ventured upon the porch and finally into the house.
Once inside, I remained quiet and from the silence came this thought: "How great it is to simply live upon the earth where our support is forever being renewed." My sole purpose from that moment on has been to further the idea of the glory of life and to tell of the beauty I find each morning with the coming of a new day.

The meaning of life is forever just beyond our grasp, but we are given tools to work with and the work we do makes all the difference. The system of Belief will always bring with it whatever we choose whether it is the creation story of an Eternal Spirit or whether one day a monkey just got lucky. I choose to believe the former for I have the power to reason, and I can plainly see that each choice comes with its very own consequence.

Making a Home

After gaining entry into the house, one of the first things I did was to build a fire out of the cob I found by the stove. Someone had eaten all the corn off of it. Soon the little house was warm, and I set about gnawing a hole through to the oustide in order to keep watch over my whereabouts. I called this my "knothole" and fashioned a stopper so I could close it up at night for the sake of safety. I soon learned that I could sit quietly by the knothole and gain a great deal of information about the neighbors. I had even put a little sign at the knothole that said "Listen and Learn" to remind me of this. Many times I could get more information if they didn't know I was there.

At this time, I did not know the knothole would lead me from the outside to the inner plane of who I am, and so it was I discovered another world within myself.

The house provided the first warmth and safety I had known, and the comfort of my very own bed was awaiting me at night with covers made of many patches. In the meadow, a pile of shavings or bit of cotton pulled out of someone else's tick was my only bed.

I do have tools to work with; they are called hands and feet and a willing mind. I could see what needed to be done as I went to work on both the inside and the outside of my house. Some of my worst habits were laid to rest, for while I was busy I seldom felt the urge to cut paper or gnaw holes, things that seemed so necessary at the time. I have made many a nest out of shredded paper and gnawed many a hole through some of the finest wood. I never knew what I would find until I was inside a cupboard.

When I first moved into the garden house, I took the name of Mattie Grey after some of my relatives. This qualified me as a respected occupant and I began overhearing folks discussing me and saying, "Mattie gnaws." I felt very good about this and handed out much advice, but as I studied, I would learn the difference between gnawing and knowing and to this day, I am still learning.

These days my work is the greatest pleasure, and my house fairly shines from the top to the bottom. Many times I will put on my white stockings to check and see if my floors are really clean, and on a sunny day I can see even one speck of dust. I had not been living here very long before I heard the house being referred to as the "Grey Place," and I took even greater care in the least detail of keeping my home. Ownership always makes a statement.

My life was so elevated after moving into the Garden House that I was able to see the source of the fear and poverty I had been running from all my life. It boiled down to two things: folks did not care for one another and they did not share. I saw much waste each day as the garden yielded up its wealth, season after season. In order to share, it was then that I designed and made an apron with four pockets; two on the outside and two on the inside to hold my gatherings, and perhaps if I was robbed my inner pockets would safeguard some of my holdings.

One of the last things I did at night, after stopping up the knothole, was to sort my pockets down to the very last pea. It was then that I learned to sort my thoughts, for to keep order in the mind thoughts cannot be allowed to run rampant.

There are many books in the Garden House, and in the early days, I was able to learn to read with the help of one of the neighbors who became a very dear friend, a Mr. Toad. I can say with all certainty that has made all

the difference. After becoming acquainted with books, I could never again cut up such priceless treasures. I read such lines as "The wild bee rang the foxglove bell." And I recall another line: "Though nothing can bring back the hour of splendor in the grass; of glory in the flower." That brings both the greatest pleasure and the greatest sadness, for it reminds me to look at each moment of life as a rare jewel and above all else to spend my time wisely for it is here today only.

Thus, the years of making a home saw many improvements and many inventions as I learned from each past experience. My knothole was the main source of the information I was gathering each day; the bits and pieces, the facts and questions. These were like the corn nuggets I saved in the jar and so the diary grew.

I learned that life does not have to be so hard, for it is largely left up to the choices we make. We are each served by our own hand.

The Garden

That first day on the porch, when I looked farther and saw a garden, I could have in no way imagined the influence it would have. Along the way, I began to see the whole earth as a garden where something is always growing.

Outside my back door, I saw more clearly the miracle of my own garden that grew not only beauty, but every bite we had to eat, as spring after spring the cycle of renewal was constant.

In the meadow we searched for food daily and tried to avoid the many traps that seemed to be set on every side. It was only when I tended a garden of my own that I saw the connection between the bloom and what would later become food. When the garden was in full bloom, I would sit for hours on the bench writing in my diary. I saw each day in a different light, as the purpose of the garden was unfolding.

Through the scope of the garden I have examined every aspect, from the first two green leaves that appear above the brown earth to the dried pod that is left hanging in the dead of winter. I have watched the flowering garden grow into food and listened to the flowing water as it rushes down the hill and into my spring box.

Water is the one substance all life depends on. In my early years I heard the expression, "making water." This was an error on the part of my ancestors, for water cannot be made but rather has been a part of the earth since the beginning. Water is in many forms, from the great polar ice to the gentle dew that gathers on the ground at night. There are springs and wells, and water runs throughout the underground. Water has great power and patiently works over long periods of time to change the landscape and even cut canyons through solid stone. The moon, the tides and the clouds are systems of watering the earth from the great storage basins, the oceans. There is also the sound of rain on the roof that brings a soothing prelude to sleep.

Water is the prime reason there is life upon the earth. We swim and bathe in water. We skate on the frozen pond in winter. Most important--we drink water and without it we would soon all die, for each of us is in large measure composed of water. The earth today is the same Garden of Eden, watered from many sources -- water that gathers again and again to fall as rain where it is needed. The blueprint of the garden is locked in a seed, and only the solvent action of water can unlock the prison-like shell to let the germ go free to grow and flourish. As gardeners we understand this. As laborers with the laws that have been set in place, we see it is from the design of the garden that everyone and everything is nourished. Today I will copy another sign to hang under the knothole: "Fields Feed the Common Man and also Kings."

Soon after gaining entry into the house of my dreams, I considered not only the beauty, but the fact that if we look after the earth, it will look after us. I began to choose habits and do everything in my power to promote and protect such a lifestyle. Cleaning and upgrading was uppermost in my mind, as I picked up trash and kept both the inside and the outside looking respectable. I even put up signs to encourage the neighbors to stop their littering. One of the signs said: "It Takes Trash to Litter." This did get some results that have lasted until this day.

The garden is bound up in seasons, as well as is everything else we know of. Seasons speak of order and design, of beauty and of reason. During the seasons of my lifetime, I have watched the constant changing of it all, the day and night, the coming in and going out, even as the tide. It is from the seasons I have heard a voice that is constant, and I never tire of the tale the seasons tell over and over.

As the twilight closes on another day, I put the knot stopper back into the hole, and in the lingering twilight go to sleep listening to my heart singing a little song all its own. It is a song of gladness at being alive through all the seasons. I then look up at the vast dome that covers us all and think about the wonders of night, whose mystery may exceed the day.

The Seasons

This morning, as spring is approaching, I filled an old canning jar with the first daffodils from the garden. I sat on the bench and felt the warm sun and marveled at the brightness of the springtime. It was in this joyous season that I first saw the true meaning of life and my relationship to it. On this morning when I was thinking about this, I threw up my hands and said out loud, "I love the whole world." It was in this moment that the glory and wonder touched my heart and mind to such an extent that I would never be the same again.

Moments such as this are stamped into the present to last forever as memory. And as the seasons passed, even the deepest snow could not muffle or drown out the song that my heart was singing. The world I discovered may be overlooked by the cares and concerns of living, even by kings. There is great beauty on every side, and every sense shouted that beauty not only decorates

the earth but supports the efforts of all we do. The plum is a white blossom before it is purple. In springtime we see the resurrection of the earth from the powers that lie in the husk of last year's seed. Seeds will lie dormant sometimes for years, only to burst into life when they meet with the right condition. Each seed is forever waiting its own time.

The ripe summer gives back to us in full measure for all our effort in planting and keeping the long rows hoed and watered and weeded. As the summer comes to an end, once again the garden has yielded up much food and everyone around here has stored away as much as we can. In the summer, I always go back to the meadow to pick berries and the flowers that grow there. Mr. Toad is very fond of blackberries and says the flowers cannot be eaten, but he is not turned toward the value of beauty. I, on the other hand, cannot measure the pleasure I get from the flowers.

Other pastimes of summer are the parties on the porch and the trips to the swimming hole. We all gather each evening after supper to sit outside to visit and watch the fireflies. The children bring their jars with lids and make a game to see who can catch the most lightening bugs. Before we go in, I see that all of the insects are set free. I tell the children that in the world of insects, they will be known as heroes for their actions. The little bugs are free now to light another night. I am hoping each child will see himself as having a role in making the world free.

The autumn comes to the year bringing us full baskets -- its trees hanging with ripe fruit and its seeds and berries all along the paths of wildlife. I see many flowers now along the road and fence lines; the goldenrod, stickweed, the royal-looking asters, the black-eyed susans and all the little weeds blooming to scatter their kind into the future. I see flower heads sitting on short stalks as if hurrying to make their seed before the winter comes. The year in the autumn gives me a merry heart and a giving spirit. I rush eagerly each day to share with anyone I meet.

On fall days we all go about gathering wood. The stove is important, and it takes much wood to do the cooking and keep us warm throughout the winter. The harvest dinner is an event to look forward to and one to remember. Aside from the cooking, a wood fire brings cheerfulness as we sit around the stove and make plans for the many celebrations we always have. The earth sees no greater show than when the Harvest Moon rises to give its pale light over the bare fields that have once again given us their crops that will carry us through the winter.

From the warm safety of my winter home, I look out upon a world of quiet splendor. Most folks do not get out unless they have to. Today I will read. Good books are a pleasure and contain thoughts that have been carried into the present from many years ago. It is sad if one does not read a little each day. Today is also a time to bake and in doing so the whole house will be warm and smell of baking bread. Everyone around can tell what is in the oven and they will all be here for a sample. Winter is a time to rest.

As the great Earth sleeps under the snow, I am reminded that to everything there is a season and life is made up of cycles. I am also very sure that the earth will turn again to spring and the foxgloves will grow and bloom again in the garden. While a storm rages across the land, all is well in the Grey house. I am preparing a feast in honor of winter. All of my biggest pots and pans are filled with the season's best, things I have cured and canned and laid up on the shelf to dry. There is great safety secured by our hard work that goes on during the other seasons. We can afford to rest and dream of how life really is in the garden and in the house and all over the land and be unafraid.

Friends and Neighbors

As I look through the knothole, I notice a family of mallards who live on a small pond near my garden. The Mallards are a happy pair except for one flaw: they did not have a family. Late in life when they had just about given up hope, Papa Mallard found a duckling. Some grand turn of fate left the duckling near the pond where the Mallards lived, so Papa took him home. Words cannot describe the happiness they felt. Nothing was too good for Duck (what they named him). He had Buster Brown suits, music boxes and everything else he asked for.

For many years, nothing ruffled a single feather in the Mallard household. Every day the great sun rose to warm and light the water and happiness grew with the days. But, as often happens in this life, tragedy struck the family with the untimely deaths of both parents in a boating accident on the pond. Duck was right back where he started at the time he was hatched from his egg. Both then and now, the world seemed a very large and frightful place. He was better off in some ways for he was the only one mentioned in the will.

Right away Duck felt the thrill of buying new things. Nothing gave him a lift like spending money, and before long he was penniless and had even lost his childhood home. He remembered some of his mother's sayings, especially when she said, "Duck, you are your own worst enemy." But the saying that bothered him the most was when she had told him that a fool and his money are soon parted. He did not feel exactly foolish, but he couldn't figure out exactly how life worked.

Each day, after his family was gone, Duck stayed on the pond as long as there was any daylight left and then he roosted in the doorway of a small, empty house that stood nearby. By and by, one day he saw smoke coming from the chimney, so he put off his bedtime until it was good and dark. Safety was his main concern, for who knows what else might happen to him.

One morning instead of going directly to the pond he decided he would peck on the door and felt the sooner he did it the better off he would be. At least he could ask if he could keep roosting in the doorway.

I knew someone was on the doorstep at night, but I could not see who it was through the knothole. I heard the pecking, and when I opened the door I felt this day as Papa Mallard must have felt when he first found the duckling. He was not quite as helpless now, but I could see that he needed me. He seemed to be cheered when I told him, "We are all in the same boat."

As time passed, one day Duck said, "I have told you things about myself that no one else knows, and sometimes I feel so grateful that tears come to my eyes when I think that you love the real me in spite of all my blundering. Things like losing the house, and that I have eaten enough corn for a large flock at nearly every meal. You have helped me face my fear of the water, after I saw what happened to my parents, and have given me the courage to swim again. You have seen inside my stout, broad-breasted body where a lonely timid soul would run to hide when life got just too painful. I used to call this place inside of me 'my duck blind.' I could get away from the world there, but I was not coping very well until that day you opened your home and heart to me. There is nothing like the healing power of concern to make a body whole again."

The more aware I am of my neighbors the more I see that we all need one another. I became friends one day with Looney Bumble on a day when he had an affair with near disaster. I had gone to pick strawberries. Looney was on his eternal quest for the nectar he gathers from the flowers. As I came near the strawberry patch, I saw a large robin hidden, she thought, in the leaves. She thinks nothing of pecking great holes in the choice berries. I watched her a while, and the moment she saw me she flew away. Folks do not like to get caught in their wrongdoing. I filled my basket with what Mrs. Robin had left and started back to the house.

As I passed the foxgloves, I heard a strange grinding noise and set the basket down to see what was going on. It took only a glance to see Looney stuck fast, deep in a bell-shaped flower. I felt great alarm and circled around trying to see what could be done to free him. Finally, without my thinking about it, my old habit of gnawing showed up. I quickly ran up the stalk and gnawed off the bloom. Looney, flower and all, fell to the ground with a soft thud. He was very grateful that I had happened by at the right time.

Life is strange, in that sometimes even a bad habit seems to serve some purpose. I remember the first time I saw Looney. He had scotched himself with one leg on the inside of a big squash blossom to keep from falling into its center. I can't help thinking Looney brings all this on himself.

Mr. Toad is a neighbor who has stood the test of time. From the first time he came to visit until this very day he has been true in all his dealings. I still remember the first time I saw him. Just as he hopped upon the doorstep, I was sweeping the house-- and with one sweep, I sent him flying far out into the yard. It was such a funny sight, I could not help laughing. Once he had regained his composure and was sure he was not hurt, he laughed too.

The least I could do now was to invite him into the house. I was more than a little uneasy as he pulled his chair close to mine and sat there staring. Some of the fear left me when I realized he had gone to sleep as soon as he got warm. I remained very still until he began to stir, and by then it was time to set the table for lunch. Mr. Toad was wearing his camel hair coat and I thought there would not be a better time to ask him to dine with me.
As Mr. Toad stirred, he batted and blinked and looked around to see where he was, for he often slept in strange places. During this first meeting, he had slept and I had studied his innocent demeanor while he was oblivious of his existence.

Mr. Toad was called "Warty," but I felt such a handsome creature needed a better name so I simply called him "Mr. Toad." And so it was as I set the table, I watched him out of the corner of my eye. From the beginning, Mr. Toad's friendship burned steady, and it has made a large ember.

At the far side of the Meadow, many toad families live in a section called Stick Weed. It is where the common stick weed grows in the fence line. Mr. Toad is from this lineage.

One of the first things I learned about him is that he is very proud of his position, his possessions and his ancestors. Many times he says he is an only child and has had many opportunities from living in the family home that goes back many generations to having had the undivided attention of his doting mother focused upon him.

The truth of the matter is they have no idea of who they are. Master Toad, as he was called in the beginning, believed the stories his mother told him, and there was the house to prove it -- the long, winding stairway, the mirror at the landing where as long as he could remember, he had studied his reflection, both coming and going. In his child's mind, he had concluded that if he had not come from Royalty, then certainly from one of the first families. Another hint was the handsome, well-bred line of his brow.

The fact that his fingers were very long was probably behind his unusual ability to play the piano that sat in the hall. Master Toad loved to play when guests came, and he wished with all his heart he could sing, but the only sound that ever came out of his throat was a rough croak.

As he stood by the mirror and pondered all his likes and dislikes, he became fairly certain that such a handsome and sensitive creature could not be a common toad from the marsh, but must surely have good blood running in his veins. After he took one last look at his reflection, his strong graceful hind legs propelled him up the winding stairway, where he hopped into his nightshirt then his bed to dream of even more wonderful things. Life is good when one thinks well of himself regardless of what anyone else may think.

One night, Master Toad's father did not come home after he had hopped out on one of his many business ventures, as he called them. No one knows what happened to him but in the morning, Master Toad's mother gave him a new title and told him he was never to mention any of this to any one. A good way to handle this would be to act as if none of it had ever happened. She changed Master to Mr. and in a way he liked this very much, but he did not understand what any of it meant, for Mattie had called him Mr. from their very first meeting.

His mother lavished even more attention on the young Mr. Toad and each time she said, "my husband is out of town" her words became more real until finally she believed he would some day return. We all wondered if she would recognize him, for there are so many toads living in the fence line now and as Ms. Crow says, "They all look alike and it would be hard to separate them."

One morning from across the Meadow came news of a universal nature. Mr. Toad's ailing mother had passed away in the night. This would be very difficult for him, for his mother had been the strongest influence on his life.

I had visited with the toads down through the years and shared many of my delicacies, especially since the mother had been ill. One dish that she seemed to relish was the broth I made from a certain stump in the meadow, also the apple cores and other things I would find in my pockets.

On these occasions, I must confess I scanned the house and the lavish furnishings that had been handed down, and wondered more than once if there might be a way to get Mr. Toad's holdings away from him. I expected many around would have the same thought now that his mother was not here to protect him. Mr. Toad would need help with running his home, for he had led a very sheltered life.

Mr. Toad has often said he did not marry because of his fondness for his mother's cooking, but actually he will eat anything. He never married because his mother would not let him associate with anyone and told him he was better.

After Mrs. Toad was laid to rest, many of the ladies of the neighborhood brought gifts of food and attempted to console Mr. Toad, but his grief lasted for a long time. By and by, we all grew accustomed to the loss and throughout this time I cared for Mr. Toad the best I could. He would come at lunchtime and I always fixed his favorite things to eat, then he would sit beside the stove and sleep.

This went on for a long time but as is the nature of things, one day Mr. Toad's grief seemed to be lifted somewhat and after lunch instead of going to sleep, he said he wanted to ask me a question. I waited and he asked if I would come and have supper with him. He said that he liked reciprocity, and I thought he had learned to cook a new dish. So I graciously accepted his invitation, not knowing what he planned to cook. It would give me a chance to look at the wonderful old cupboard. Also, I needed a break from the cooking chores and when Mr. Toad had seated me in the best chair, he said that was exactly what he meant.

The evening was a success by any measure and when it was over he walked as far as the gate and asked in his deepest voice if I would like to visit again. He said he would build a fire and that I would be welcome to look inside the cupboard. He added that the cupboard was probably the oldest and best piece he had.

The pleasant days and visits continued and as the seasons changed into years, I came to realize what a grand character Mr. Toad really has. I also came to see that his mother's influence had, in a large measure, helped him to become the toad that he is. As we became friends, I came to depend on his many acts of kindness. I remember one of the first gifts: it was a sugar bowl made of the heaviest cut glass. He said it was a favorite of his mother's and that he believed she would want me to have it.

The bringing of gifts is one of Mr. Toad's greatest pleasures, and before long I realized he had moved most of his fine family pieces into the Garden House, where I have lived now for a good while. Most of what was here was quite ratty looking, and Mr. Toad said he thought I was deserving of something better.

Early one morning, I remembered the cupboard. I had not thought of it in a long time for I did have a house full of wonderful things by then; but feeling a little greedy, I wished I could have the cupboard also and hoped I could remember to ask about it that very day, which I did.

Mr. Toad said, "Mattie, I know the cupboard is perhaps the best piece my family accumulated. . .and I have no use for such things now. . .and I would have given the cupboard to you a long time ago but for the fact that it is too tall. . .and I have never been able to bring myself to saw it in two. . .but this morning before I left the house, I moved it out from the wall and got the ladder and the saw ready. It's funny you would ask about the cupboard this day. It means we were both thinking of the same thing and it must be the truth about great minds. I want you to come home with me to hold the ladder."

I could scarcely take in what his words indicated and could only manage to whisper, "Have you made the first cut?"

When he said, "No, the ladder is rickety and some of the rungs are altogether missing," I heaved a sigh of relief.

Mr. Toad stood staring, as he often does, and I had a few minutes to recover. So as to try not to appear too anxious about the cupboard, I said, "Mr. Toad, I have been thinking of building a Tower."

Many times, by changing the subject, I have had complete control over whatever mind he may have. I soon saw that this was certainly true that day, for Mr. Toad hopped right on the idea and said he would go fetch the ladder and his new saw. I said I had been thinking of it awhile, because I had found out just about all I could from looking through the knothole and was fairly certain I could understand a lot more if I could see from a tall Tower exactly what was going on with each of the neighbors and had even run a name over in my mind -- it would be called "The Tower of Knowledge." I have to admit the most pressing thought was that a tin-topped Tower would accommodate the wonderful tall cupboard; at last it would be mine.

I do not really know how long Mr. Toad stood there staring, for as he often told me, most of the time that expression meant that he was asleep and sometimes even on his feet. I felt no need to put this off, so I sent Mr. Toad back home to fetch the ladder and the saw and we went immediately to the east side of the Garden House and laid the cornerstones that would support and uphold the Tower of Knowledge. I said "Dear Mr. Toad, we will move the cupboard as soon as the Tower is finished."

Another dear neighbor is Mrs. Crow. I will never forget the first time I saw her up close. I have had an unreasonable fear of her since my earliest memory in the Meadow. Back then I heard many tales that sent shocks of terror through me. This morning as I was setting the table for lunch, I heard a pecking on the outside and hurried to the knothole to investigate.

When I removed the stopper, there stood Ms. Crow with her level gaze as sharp as her beak. I did not have time to make a plan of any kind, rather my whole body reacted in one motion. I took a heel of bread out of one of my pockets and threw it through the knothole.

Some of my presence of mind came back to me as Ms. Crow said with a grateful gobble, "Thank you," and practically swallowed the bread whole. She said she had not been able to find anything to eat for several days. In sympathy, my heart went out to her and I invited her to come and dine with me. "Ms. Crow, I have a special jar that I keep only corn in and if you will come back at suppertime, I am always willing to share. I save the corn kernel by kernel and usually keep a jar full. By saving what many times other folks throw away, I can usually make good use of my findings and many times feel that I am helping with world hunger."

Ms. Crow said "thank you" again and went on her way. I sat at the hole for a long time, thinking about our encounter, and tried to reenact the fear but it had lost a great deal of its power. Hadn't she been grateful and hadn't she been hungry? I had never known if my fear of Ms. Crow was because she was so big or because she was black and, to tell the truth, I had never even thought about this before. It was always just at the mention of her name that I became fearful. Ms. Crow did come back at suppertime, and as she ate the corn in a more civilized manner, we had time to exchange a few polite words. It was the beginning of a true friendship that has grown through the years.

Ms. Crow was one of the first neighbors I met after I moved here. I tell her often that I love each of my neighbors for who they really are. It was not long after my first close-up encounter with Ms. Crow that Mr. Toad asked if we might have a special dinner in honor of the friendship and that is how it came about that the three of us ate together most days at lunchtime.

As time passed we invited many others. I am the happiest when planning, cooking and serving the meals. It takes a lot of work but it gives me a chance to use the good dishes and decorate the whole house.

By this time, Mr. Toad had carried nearly everything he owned to the Garden House, so we could celebrate in style! Ms. Crow was interested in the cooking and Mr. Toad continued to gather in the wood. His job was a lot easier now that he owned the saw. On occasion, things would not be seasoned just right, but I could usually compensate, like when Ms. Crow put apple juice in the slaw instead of vinegar. We laughed a lot and were thankful for our food and the time we spent together. Many times I wondered if it was even possible to teach a crow to cook.

The table talk sometimes was about change. Mr. Toad said he'd already made many changes and was comfortable with the way he was. Ms. Crow flatly stated she hated change and said her ancestors had mapped the shortest route to the cornfield from where they lived and neither did she like to lose time, so she would do it the old way, and added being first to the cornfield sometimes makes a difference as to whether or not you have anything to eat that day.

Ms. Crow's home is crowded with no place to sit. Once when she asked me there I remained standing, for to sit down would have been dangerous. She had carried in so many odds and ends, especially pieces of glass in many colors. Like Mr. Toad, she brings gifts to the Garden House and I never know what to do with any of them. One day I had the idea to give them back to her. I do appreciate Ms. Crow's generosity and she always seems grateful to get her pieces back so this works out for both of us.

Ms. Crow is black and beautiful and to be perfectly honest, I have had to work hard not to be envious of many of her attributes. Her ability to fly almost defies comprehension. It is no wonder Ms. Crow has the command of knowledge she does. Many times when she is telling of something she has seen, I remind her that if I could fly, I would have seen this also. Her flying does save steps and since her race is known for its longevity, she has assured me that she will always be here and do what she can to support and uphold the friendship we enjoy that seems to be cemented more securely each year.

These are no doubt the dearest words in any language to hear that someone cares and someone will help. To rely on is one thing, but to lean on when it comes to that is the greatest support that can ever be offered. Ms. Crow is that kind of friend.

Every day after lunch, I noticed Mr. Toad getting very still. He would sit by the stove and look straight ahead. By now I was familiar with his stare but this was something else. I had been reading about positive thought and the power of the mind when its energies are concentrated, and I was fascinated by the thought that perhaps Mr. Toad had encountered such in his upbringing, for he is the only one of us who has been to school. One day I thought it was time to find out.

I was fascinated by the meaning of Mr. Toad's actions so when he seemed to be aware, I asked if he had heard of positive thought or knew anything about resting his mind. He said he had not heard of anything like that, and that when he sat by the fire, it was his nap time and that toads sleep with their eyes open and he had never been aware of having a brain. I did not pursue this any further but rather asked if he would like to go sit on the garden bench awhile. He loved to sit in the garden and at these times he would show me the cuts and how he had used the saw to make such a handsome bench.

Other friends along the way were the groundhogs, Whitman and Gertrude Waddles, who moved underneath the Garden House one fall to hibernate. When the Waddles first came for the winter, I thought it would be the end of any sleep for me. Whitman snored, and I knew this would go on all winter.

One night I had the idea to count his breathing, and it worked like a charm. From that time on four breaths was all I ever heard for by that time I was fast asleep myself. It was a time I learned that it didn't matter whose breath you count; the end result of relaxation is the same.

There were few problems except for the occasional nibbling in the garden at night. I have learned to set a rock over their doorway and remove it before daylight. That way, they have each day to eat the tender grass and the garden is saved. Gertrude and Whitman are very fond of the summer fruit, especially ripe peaches and cantaloupe. They both have a weight problem, but I find it hard to find an opening to mention this. One day, I did ask Gertrude if she was a positive person and if she had made many changes in her life. About the positive, she said that for a long time she had not been able to find a string long enough to go around herself and she added, "Therefore I know I'm gaining and that is always a positive sign." I did not mention this again.

Early one year when Whitman and Gertrude came out from under the house, I noticed Gertrude had lost a lot of weight. Any change must be investigated so I did not put this off. In former days they both waddled to walk; in fact that is how they got their name. When I asked about the weight loss Gertrude said: "This past fall when we went in for the winter Whitman said to me 'Fat keeps us apart.' It was a very hurtful statement. I did not know that he even noticed this, and I made a vow to myself to lose the weight, for I did not want to lose Whitman. I used to get up at night and stumble into the kitchen and eat everything I could get my hands on. I was also eating all day during the summer months. Once I saw what I was doing wrong the rest was easy; it is always easy for the world to see."

She added, "Whitman and I have never been closer and that is worth many changes." Now when we sit on the garden bench together I always give them salad things from the garden to take home and many times peaches from my pockets. They were also invited several times a year to the celebrations that were ongoing at the garden house.

I have met a lot of folks and most of them through the knothole. One morning, as I was preparing to remove the stopper and take my seat at the hole, I thought of all the sad parades I had watched. There had also been many amusing and happy ones. The memory of this story haunts me to this day. Through the knothole I saw the skinniest cat I had ever seen. When anyone of the cat family is around it gets my full attention, so I took in every detail.

Cats sometimes fall upon hard times when they are carried a long distance from home and left in strange and hostile neighborhoods. This is referred to as being "dropped."

My family and the common housecat have never been on good terms to say the least, so I remained very still as I watched. There was a sense of urgency about this beautiful gold-and-black-striped cat that was standing right on the outside of the knothole and looking me square in the eye. During these few seconds, I saw the naked truth of what happens when one gets down on their luck to the point of not having anything to eat. It is the eye that reveals the truth.

I made a vow to myself long ago that I would never stop until there was not one homeless and hungry soul upon the entire face of the earth, so I couldn't remain silent any longer. I simply said, "I have food in the cupboard and I am willing to set a table outside."

After a small silence the cat said, so as not to appear deceitful, "I have three little kittens hidden in the bushes. I will go get them."

When I first laid eyes on the kittens, I was smitten. The cat said, "This is Ticin, Battin, and Squintin." It was obvious they all had a little something wrong with their eyes. I knew she was aware of the problem, so I said: "What they need now is warm milk and a soft bed. We will see the doctor tomorrow, and he will be able to tell at a glance if the problems are coming from too much kin in the blood." If this is the case, the next generation always has to pay the price.

I was prepared to take the family in; what I was not prepared for was the story the cat was about to tell me. It is a grave crime for even one child to be harmed, and the punishment should fit the crime. These crimes are hard to detect, but I believe if we all work together these criminals can be uncovered and the broken children could be mended. This is the only way the next generation is ever going to be sound.

Many times I had seen evidence of something in a mother's heart that stands alone, and I was seeing it again as I watched the mother feed the babies before she would eat one bite. I thought the love for the kittens would be a foundation on which to build, and I believed my actions could make a difference. Perhaps this day would be a beginning where folks would stop trying to destroy one another. Hopefully, I could show the half-starved cat how to live and let live.

I have always believed there is some good in everyone, and I know for sure that the bad can be changed. I put the family up in a small room at the back of the house and paid special attention to their diet. The kittens had warm milk every night at bedtime and soon ate from the table, also. All babies are innocent, and the kitten antics amused and brought joy to us all.

During this time we had many conversations through the knothole. In the beginning I told of how I'd learned to support myself and help many others by being willing to work. Of course, I did not know where success comes from either, but as I put into practice what I knew, other advances were revealed to me. My actions said to the cat, "You are welcome to stay here and share in all that I have until you are back on your feet, and then if you are willing I will show you a way to have a successful journey throughout all the days of your life."

We all live in a world that replenishes itself daily and is ever ready to serve us. One thing I stressed to the cat was the idea that when I looked deep enough inside myself, I always saw that we are all much the same and a common thread seems to connect us all.

As the cat listened to my many discourses on the nature of the animal and the universe, she regained her strength and had an inner glow that came from pure happiness and the pride she felt as she watched the kittens learn and grow in the shelter of a good home.

One day the cat asked if she might have an audience in order to tell her story. She began by saying: "We all have a story. I can see myself in the children I am trying to raise on my own. Being a single parent poses many problems but sometime the hardships are better than what happens to many of us as children. Our neighborhood was very much like any other on the surface of things but in many ways we were different. I feel like my mother had high hopes for me, for before she knew of the eye problems, she had given me the name 'China Rose.'

"My mother worked hard to support us, and she was not at home much of the time. When she was at home there would always be 'friends,' as she called them, hanging out and there was always someone asleep on the woodpile. One day as I played near the woodpile something happened that I was at a loss to understand. I was to learn later that the same thing had happened to many of the others.

"Looking back, I am sure my mother knew about this. I guess she felt it would cause too big a stir to mention it. I remember her talking about her friends being on the prowl. I thought it was their place of employment. This mistreatment continued throughout my early years. At first, I had nightmares and other strange behavior patterns, like sleepwalking. I was fearful all the time and did not cope well. I was told that the abuse was a secret and the secret meant that we get along well. It was many years before I was able to know the truth.

"When I was a teenager, I discovered another secret, and by this time I knew what the secret meant, for I was now going to be a mother myself. This was another painful time in my life. I knew if I stayed there, my family would be facing the same tragic circumstance. So one day while my mother was at work, I left my childhood home and put as many miles as I could walk between where I was going and the home I was leaving. There are many single parents for many reasons and I pledge on my honor that I will take your message as far as I go and like you, I will somehow make a difference in my own lifetime."

My heart was touched by this sad story.. I know just the kind of cat she had reference to. They are carnivores with 20/20 vision, they disregard everything except their appetite and they are very hard to get away from. As the kittens grew, in due time, the cat family moved into a bigger place, but to this day I get cards with little messages reminding me that they remember the happy time at the garden house and what a difference it had made.

One spring morning, I met another neighbor as I was gathering the early greens along the road. He was an Irish potato bug, traveling in the opposite direction. I called out to him, but there was not the slightest pause so I turned and ran to catch up with him. I marveled at his speed on his thin legs and large body. I have taken an interest in everyone around and have a large store of facts about all the folks who live far and near so I asked him, "Where are you from and where are you going?"

He responded: "I am known as O'Neil. I came from Ireland, and now I am a resident of the United States of America. I have been lonely and wished many times I could get back to my former home; they say you can't go back, but I have tried. I am now on my way to Clarence's potato patch to eat the vines and I must get there before they are dusted. The sickest I can ever remember being was after eating the leaves that had a product called Sevin on them. It is hoped that someone had dusted the leaves by mistake, but one can never be too careful.

"Back in my country, at one time I was known as 'The Potato Bug.' After accidentally falling out of a cuff, I traveled all the way here on a boot, trying to escape the great Irish potato famine. I have worked hard and I feel America truly is a land of opportunity for anyone who will get up early."

I watched as he crossed under the fence and into the vines. As I went back to gathering the early spring greens, I thought about what it means to be patriotic and also that in a sense we are all immigrants.

As I think of O'Neil's story, I feel sad that he has been cut off from his family. All of my neighbors have stories to tell and I remember O'Neil's words as he recounted his life: "My home is on the side of a steep mountain, and many times I tried to walk to the top of the mountain for I believed Ireland to be at the top. I am a good walker and many of those times I made it almost to the top, but always I missed it by some distance. I could never tell just how far. So through the years, I trudged up and down the mountain always hoping the next time I'd make it to Ireland.

"With this daily routine my health grew into a robust state. I cannot say the same for my home on the mountainside, for by this time it was in shambles from sheer neglect. But season by season, I walked and finally one early autumn afternoon, I stood on the top of the mountain. I was shocked to my very heels for I saw that Ireland was not where I thought it was. I had been mistaken, but what I was confronted with nearly took my breath away. It was a lake with a sign that said 'The Top of the World,' and I thought to myself what a fitting name.

"I ventured very close, in fact to the very edge of the water, where my reflection looked back at me. I stood there spellbound for I saw a very special looking fellow, and in those few moments I knew I had found a friend. I stood there looking at someone I had so longed to be close to and it became clear I had been looking in the wrong direction and perhaps all that I had walked and searched for was closer than I imagined.

"As the sun was setting, I retraced my steps down the mountain, which always took less effort than the many attempts I had made to get to the top. I had a lot to think about on this lovely autumn evening, so I decided to put my house in order while I relived my mountaintop experience. I also planned to go there again.

"First I made a plan. On Tuesday I would renew all my pillows and repair the broken threads in the beautiful embroidery and hang clean curtains. Some of the other days were spent in scrubbing, polishing and general maintenance and upkeep until the little house gleamed in the glow of the soft sunsets. In the following days, I felt a certain contentment within myself and one day suddenly remembered it had been a week since I'd seen my reflection in the water and not once had I felt the terrible longing for someone or some place that I could never quite find.

"On the next trip, I discerned that when I did not dissipate my energies it was easier. Instead of every day, I would only go once a week and the other days I would take up matters pertaining to my personal up-building (myself and my home). As I put this plan into action my days became better. At last I felt

very complete and sure of things inside myself, my home and my country, and that Ireland was mostly a state of mind. I am still living on the same steep rural road that leads to the mountaintop where peace and beauty reign. When I learned to look in the right direction, I found that those things could be mine every day, and I could still go to Ireland on Sunday."

I was greatly relieved as I realized that O'Neil had come to grips with his life in this country, and I wished I had been there to welcome him from the first. America once said to the world: "Give me your lonely, your weary crowded masses, the hordes composed of many classes, the starved and frayed; come I will take you in and you will see, life does flourish when it's safe and free." I don't believe we still go by the meaning of these words but the need for them is even greater.

One day as I watched the summer harvest, all the folks who live among the stick weeds along the fence line had gathered to cut the cane. The cane crop is valuable, for it satisfies the sweet tooth we all have. Actually, I believe it is the tongue that needs to be sweetened, for it is the tongue alone that seems to scatter the seeds of bitterness and discontent.

I have time now to think about this, and one day soon I intend doing a serious study about why the tongue is such a destructive instrument. I often watch Ms. Crow and listen to her ideas.

I also have learned from long study that in silence the whole universe will reveal the truth to us. In these moments, I wonder why Ms. Crow never ceases her quest for new ideas and new objects, but to get back to the knothole, I had all I could do that day to keep up with all that was going on in the cane field.

As the morning wore on, the day was very hot, for the sun was directly overhead. Something had happened to O; that is the neighborhood's name for the opossum. He was on the ground. I could not account for that, for it is a well-known fact that O can cut more cane than all the other workers. It is also a well-known fact that O has the sharpest and the most teeth of anyone living in the fence row, now or at any other time.

I had noted long ago that everyone has some characteristic that sets him apart from his neighbor, and it is the teeth alone that shine in a perpetual grin that shows where the strength of the possum lies.

There was no sign of life as the others crowded around, fanning and pouring water over O, after dragging him into the shade. Presently, someone remembered Uncle Toad and the rumor that he was a handler of the dead. There are always rumors, and way back some of Uncle Toad's ancestors had been accused of handling more than the dead. Uncle Toad, a relative of Mr. Toad, had long ago moved from the fence line into town, where he has a flourishing business as the undertaker. Aside from the rumors, none of us knew anything about him. We did know that Uncle Toad drives his own van with the letters U.T. on his license plate.

At one time Uncle Toad was well-loved, but after he moved away, he seemed to have little dealings with folks unless they were in O's apparent condition. Whatever they didn't know, O was about to find out. They did know it was urgent to get some kind of help, so one of Ms. Crow's nephews offered to get word to the undertaker, as he was called in town. In no time at all, the

long van rolled into the cane field, and O was carefully lifted into the back of it. Uncle Toad sped off as fast as the rutted field would allow him.

Some time passed between the trip from the cane field to the time some of O's senses began to return to him. At first he remained very still and tried to understand what was going on around him and kept his eyes tight shut. Presently, he was forced to peep, for pure panic was welling up inside of him and it took every power he possessed to look and try to see where he was and what was happening to him or about to happen. He had felt the undertaker working with his arms and legs, as if trying to find something.

When he summoned enough strength to look, there was Uncle Toad with a slender knife in one hand and with the other hand finding out where to make a cut. There was a foul-smelling liquid on a tray and a very bright light overhead. O had never before felt such naked terror.

O has told his story many times and always says it was not thought that enabled him to escape but a reflex that only his muscles knew about, with the help of his teeth. One of the undertaker's hands was near the teeth, and in a blinding second, one of the fingers was completely severed from the hand. It was now Uncle Toad's time to stare in disbelief, for his blood was flowing freely. As for O, it was all in one motion that he fled the scene that day, and he did not stop running until he reached his home among the stick weeds.

O never ceased to explain what he had learned firsthand about Uncle Toad's business, and he warned everyone never to go near there as long as they had any of their senses about them. As for Uncle Toad, the loss of his finger was very unfortunate, but his hand did heal and he is still able to handle his equipment. One day when he was examining the wound he thought to himself, "I guess I am lucky for in all this time and large volume of business, O is the first live one I have ever got hold of, or maybe I should say, whoever got hold of me."

Bundles of Bunnies

True friendship comes without the excess baggage that many other relationships bring. I have seen ties of friendship that outlast ties of family relationships. The relationship I have with Minnie rabbit is such a friendship. She and her family live in the root system of a large elm tree that was the home also of a rabbit of old, named Peter. They all originate from that line. The home is underneath the corncrib, and the massive tree gives them shelter and shade.

Minnie has a large family, and with a lot of children there come a lot of grandchildren. She never tires of telling about them, especially the youngest grandchild, whose name is James. James is a soft round rabbit whose big innocent eyes look at the world with wonder. Everyone around loves James, and we all take turns babysitting.

One day when Minnie and I were in the yard, Ms. Crow lit in our midst to visit awhile. I was grateful to see Ms Crow, for something on the stove was burning. As I finished the cooking, I could hear parts of their conversation drifting back and forth through the knothole.

Minnie was saying: "I wonder sometimes what will become of us. I have children and grandchildren. Mattie will be fine as long as she is able to keep up the silly, elaborate parties, but take away the tablecloth and all the food she is forever fixing and things may not be the same. Her table is filled with decoration to the point it looks like a southern belle flaunting her wares. There are finger bowls, salt cellars, placemats and place cards and more dishes on the table than there is food. You have to sit straight up and handle your food in a certain manner. It is no wonder stress at mealtime causes heartburn and gas. It would be a horror indeed if one should hiccup or sneeze.

"Wisdom is lacking here, for large portions of rich food, especially at bedtime have many consequences. The appetite allowed to run wild is very dangerous. Mr. Toad is a fair example of what eating too much will cause. Lately there is work going on at the Grey house that she says is her best idea yet. It will be a Tower so she can see farther than she ever has. Building such a thing will only make more steps to climb. I would much rather live in the ground. I see the total waste of time and energy, but I learned long ago to agree with whatever plans folks may have for two reasons. First, none of us want the same thing; and second, to disagree would dampen the friendship. I am looking forward to visiting her in the Tower if I am able to hop up that far by the time it is finished. Mr. Toad does have the new saw, and he does everything in his power to please her, so the Tower may go up without delay.

"But to get back to things that are common to our family, we are a timid bunch and rather than to confront matters, we will usually run. Running has saved many a rabbit. I have lived to an advanced age by running from trouble. Perhaps the fact that I feel great happiness has something to do with my age. I do not dwell on such things though, for I have always felt that being happy is a mystery.

"I have been very happy this day for I have worked on a job that I dearly love; it is the running of my Singer. In the buzz of bobbins and thread, cogs and wheels, I am doing what I do best which is running the sewing machine that makes the little fancy clothes that all the children wear for Easter. Just now in the drone of the motor, I thought about my early life and how I came to be such an expert in one of my professions.

"To be considered wise, one must fill the mind with many notions, but in the beginning my intent was to clothe our family and perhaps bring home a little pay that would ease the burdens of my own Mother, who had so many to take care of. Back then, it always fell to the women of the family to somehow make it all work. So at an early age I sought work at a sewing factory. It turned out to be a job that I loved, and before long I was laying out patterns that I drew myself and also working on the machines when one of them would break down. This happened so often that soon I did nothing else but take the machines apart, clean and oil the parts, and when I put them back together they ran like new. I was doing well for a girl but did not get any more pay, and nothing was ever said about advancement. As I was tracing all of this today, I thought of something I did as a child. My mother would let me take a clock apart when it would no longer keep time, and as I searched the parts, many times I could get it to tick again. I guess in childhood, many things either help or hurt.

"In addition to sewing, I also learned to weave little baskets for the children to carry. Many years ago, so long that I have lost track of the meaning, something happened that had to do with James' grandfather being called the Easter bunny. It fell to him, he said, to tell the Easter story and deliver eggs to children all over the world. In the beginning, I made the frocks and wove the baskets, but it was soon apparent that I could only do so much, so he went on with what he called his life's work without me. I stayed home and took care of the family and enjoyed running the sewing machine.

"There were many at that time interested in the idea of Easter. I am fairly certain that wherever he is he can get the job done, for his nature was charming and persuasive. On occasion, I think of him, but I cannot remember exactly what he looked like, and at these times I say to myself it is just as well that I did not hold onto that dream any longer than I did, for his lifestyle was not going anywhere.

"I see many traits in James that remind me of his grandfather. Even so, I am very protective of him and do not take lightly when he is taken advantage of in any way. I guess being overprotective is a trait most mothers and grandmothers have. When James was little, he developed an illness I called 'the knee jerk.' After watching James at this, I decided he was reacting to something, and as I thought about this, I came to believe James was confused by life in general by not having a grandfather. This body language is, I believe, an attempt of the body to express the unrest that remains at the core of our being until it is dealt with.

"These symptoms are not peculiar to childhood, for without the proper treatment, I see it going on in people of all ages. At the time I knew little about these symptoms, but I knew I could ask Mattie what was causing James to shake his legs and many times his whole body. She said, 'You have named it right. I have recognized these symptoms and studied them at length. If you will bring James to the Tower when it is finished, I will get to the bottom of whatever is working on him, and he will be all right. Minnie, there are a multitude of symptoms the body will call into play when it is seeking a cure.'

"James cannot run very fast yet, and he often walks in the red squirrel's foot steps. One day on their walk they found some ears of corn that someone had carried that far and dropped. The red squirrel works hard at storing food for winter, so he  told James if he would stand guard over the corn until he could carry all the kernels home he would give him the cobs when he got down to them. James agreed, for he did not know the difference. In due time, James picked up his empty cobs and started toward home. The red squirrel had told him of all the uses of corncobs and James believed him, for he remembered that I needed the cobs for kindling.

"James was trusting, and when I heard about his day, I hugged him and thought it is no wonder we are called dumb bunnies, but I never said anything. However, I did think about the labels that are thrust upon us and the hidden life we each are privileged to build. In my case I have worked and studied to ensure the safety of future generations by teaching the children all I have gleaned from those who have gone before.

"I had picked blackberries that day and of course we always had an abundance of corn. I was aware that I must teach James more about the ways of the world. The red squirrel will learn maybe someday that even a little deceit will make a body ill, but he may live most of his life in this deceitful manner. James can look forward to a good life, for having a family makes all the difference. So as to make James feel better about himself, I showed him where I had stopped a hole here and there with a cob to keep out the winter cold. And while I was at it, I took James outside and showed him the pile of ashes I had collected when I cleaned the grates. I told him about making soap with the lye that was an end product when water is run through wood ashes. James will need to know these things when the time comes for him to take his place in the world.

"Ms. Crow, am I boring you? But as I was saying, as James began growing to young manhood he often wanted to go out at night, but I spoke to him of the many dangers. He felt he had learned about all of those things, so one night when the moon was full, James gave in to the temptation he was feeling to discover what was above his home in the great outdoors. Shortly after bedtime, he left the house, unbeknown to me.

"I would learn later that James did not spend that night alone. That was the night he got home a little before daylight and roused me out of a sound sleep, saying he planned to get married and had made up his mind during the night. I rubbed the sleep from my eyes and was interested and sat up all in one motion. My first thought was I had beads and lace and satin enough to make a wedding gown, and later I thought of making a jacket for James. All this day was a stir in the house under the corncrib. In the evening there came a small knock on the back door. I knew it was Mattie Grey, for lately she had come this time of evening to keep us informed of the progress being made on the Tower."

When I saw all the rabbits sitting around the table and it not even being meal time, I knew something was up and asked if I might come and sit a while. Minnie is not one to keep secrets so she said, "Please come in and have a seat. James is getting married and out of necessity it must be as soon as the arrangements can be made."

I was beside myself with glee when I found out what was going on and thought if I were to build a fire under Mr. Toad, the Tower could be ready by the next day. The bride would be just as graceful hopping up the stairs as she would be hopping down them. Minnie rabbit said firmly: "She will come down the stairs. James and the rest of us will wait in the garden. I have my heart set on a wedding in the garden and I insist that it take place there. I am also determined that James will get some of this right! And as far the Tower goes, you can plan another celebration when it is finished."

I love celebrations, and I also love the groom who used to be the soft round rabbit who sat on my knee, so immediately I invited James to spend his honeymoon in the Tower. Since this would take some getting ready, I told the rabbits good night and hurried back to the Garden House to get the Tower ready for a honeymoon. As I drifted off to sleep this night I had one final thought, "They will surely allow me to hold the reception!"

After the excitement of the wedding, James and his bride settled in the Meadow to take up living on their own. Minnie continued to learn all she could so she could pass on the rules that would ensure the safety and well-being of her family. She often said how important her grandchildren were and that she wanted to teach them all the things that she had taught James. They needed to become wise and learn what it means to take care of what the Earth provides and make sure it would pass to the next generation as it had been passed to them. She told me that many days as she settled in and ran the sewing machine, she thought it was great to be a grandmother, and it crossed her mind that there could very well be great grandchildren under the corncrib before long.

Lessons Learned

Visiting is the height of pleasure and I love to dress up on these occasions. I usually visit on rainy days when I cannot get outside to do anything. My colorful rainwear keeps me dry and the big umbrella gives me a lift. As I step out into the yard, I breathe the water-scented air and look at the flowers that hold their cupfuls of sparkling drops.

On this particular day, I had packed my pockets with a variety of things, for I never know who I might run into. I planned to check on a family I had not heard anything of since they moved.

When I arrived, instead of knocking on the door, I walked on toward the barnyard. I wanted to see George, the rooster, again. When I was part of the way through the gate he greeted me with a voice that vibrated the very ground he stood on and even seemed to reach into the sky. He said "I am only crowing and I am famous for this." He added, almost as an afterthought, "I get the sun up. Nothing has ever happened to make me think otherwise. In the early morning darkness, as soon as I have crowed, there is always a faint light in the East, followed by the rising of the sun."

I looked at George and thought, "That's it. Belief, standing right in front of me." It was a thought that overran the boundaries of anything I had ever considered before, and for the moment was as far as I could go. I decided I would take this up again after I had moved into the Tower, for there alone I can work on unraveling such a staggering concept.

Belief is the first cause, and I said to myself, "So, that's it. Life is a mind game."

I emptied the contents of my pockets for the flock, and looked one last time at the massive barn that is such a storehouse against the Winter. I remembered the bales, barrels and bins, for I have lived in many a barn and know of the morsels hidden there. In the past I have noticed also the fact that a great deal of life's nuggets in general seem to be hidden from us.

I looked again at George surrounded by his ladies in waiting, and admired their beauty that decorates the farmyard, to say nothing of the nutritional egg that is packaged in such a safe manner that goes a long way toward nourishing the world. They were all there: Henny Penny, Chicken Little, The Little Red Hen, and Goldie the large hen that lays the egg with the double yolk, and Merrifeather whose beauty stands alone. I watched as George offered first one, and then another, a choice tidbit he'd unearthed with his toe.

I had a mind to come back that night, after they had all gone to roost and have a few morsels myself. In olden times there were a lot of henhouse raids at night. I have lived well, though, on the grains, apples and other vegetations, so I would never be interested in a chicken dinner. It is the barn that I had my eye on.

I bade them goodbye and backed out of the gate. As I walked on toward home with a lively gait, I said out loud more to myself than to anyone who might be listening, "He really believes he can get the sun up."

I thought I must get back to the Garden House and record this in my diary and in permanent ink at that. I am onto something big, and now that the Tower is all but complete, I will know for sure if I am right.

I once had an idea to preach a sermon through the knothole in an attempt to tell of the help I have found in my daily round of living. So the sign beside my knothole would simply say, "A Sermon on Sunday," by Mattie Grey.

The topic of my sermon was "Questioning our Condition." I had put up signs about littering and obesity and hinted about the cruelties I had watched going on between folks who are supposed to be neighbors, neighbors who all display a charming outer surface. My condition is where my sermon was coming from, and when I realized others are burdened with the condition also, I thought it might help if I shared how I have made such a painful climb out of the doldrums of life and into the life I am now living.

I think maybe it starts with respect for the Earth and each other to a degree that we are willing to change our ways in order to help first ourselves and then those around us. Work is so important, for in working the necessities of life are met and always the excess to share.

In my case, there was the horde of negatives, as I named them, that had gained entry into my being. They are a destructive bunch that come from a place called "Turmoil." The negatives have names we all are familiar with; they are the cant's, the won'ts and the don'ts, whose personalities are made up of envy, greed, resentment, rebellion, lust, and hate -- to name some of them. They are strong, crafty and real, and many times they gain a stronghold before we are even aware of being infested with them.

The negatives in our lives cause the indecision, stress, and unhappiness that are responsible for many of the ills we bring upon ourselves. I am convinced there is a remedy for most of these ills in the three words, "I am sorry." We are all coded with the heavy armor of self-deception, and I had to see this before I could help myself.

There are always two sides, and this negative condition has another side. It is the positive side, and it contains every imaginable tool to build with. Any dream that we can imagine is possible.

One day, as I sat in the garden, I looked at the bench, now weathered and gray and it brought back many happy memories. Like the bench, we too have many storms to weather, but storms always pass and the joy in living goes on. As the years have taken shape, there was a moment I was sitting on this very bench when I looked through the knothole from the opposite direction and realized it is not in the world but inside ourselves that the greatest discoveries are made. In a flash of understanding, I realized I had been looking in the wrong direction. From then on I saw this moment as the building block of my future.

There are many defining moments in our lives. There was another moment when, looking through the knothole, I became aware of how small my view of life really was. As I sat there going over the prospect of how we may elevate and enlarge our lives, naturally I thought of business, for it is from business that we look for the increase.

Many times when I am very still, I will have thoughts of a revealing nature. This was such a moment, for I thought of the business of fault-finding. Fault-finding is perhaps the largest business in the world, with the least pay. Most of us have engaged in it at some time, even if just as a sideline. It is a thriving business that takes little to start. We do not need any capital or strength of character or talent or self-sacrifice, and it does not require one to have a sound mind. Being blind and deaf does help, for these conditions hide from us the make-up of human nature. The business of fault-finding is never productive, but life will always leave its largest bundle at the door of the uncomplaining-- those who have good will toward others.

In the realm of thought there was the positive equation I had discovered and called a Giant named "Yes." I saw that it would be far more profitable for me to give up my fascination with everyone who passed my knothole and actually seal up the hole. I would then have time to study change. Perhaps living in a Tower, I could see where change comes from, for I realized a better view of what the neighbors were doing could not help me. It would now be left up to me to fix my own broken parts.

It was not long after this until a difference began to show up in the diary. As I read and thought of these changes, it was evident that to get out of a rut, there has to be a road built on a higher elevation.

In the narrow confines of life, there is the design of the heart -- a vessel, a storehouse for love and compassion. In my limited time I have found in the uncharted regions of my mind an attitude that has the attributes of a giant. He is the same giant that lived once upon a time; he is still alive here and now and as able as ever.

LIFE

Life is like a collection of short stories, filled with beauty, fame and glory
Mystery bound without an end, love and turth and hope will blend
A brotherhood of foe and friend
And make of it what we may; it does not fade with the light of day,
A pearl from wisdom's knowing hand, emotion is a gift to man.
Wrapped in the senses most sublime; I pinch the mint and step briefly in the thyme.
I close my eyes and trust my senses as a guide.
Royal purple bows at dusk to lavender in the twilight sky
The splendor we are familiar with is revealed again to every eye.
At night the planets blaze and flare, the 'music of the spheres' fills the air.
Vibrations from the turning earth; the wind chimes of the universe.
My mind is on the highest peak where the music peals and swells,
And my heart is a cathedral where gratitude dwells.
As the pages have been turned and some truth of life uncovered
I have had a glimpse into the beauty I've discovered.
Life is a tale with many breaches, for habit has its well worn tracks,
But hope can read between the lines, as beauty crowds between the cracks.
And from the book that I have read
Truth stood up and boldly said
"Beauty is sustaining, as well as bread."

Tonight I will put the knot stopper back into the hole for the last time, for in the morning I will move into the Tower, and Mr. Toad will come and seal up the hole. I knew when I decided to build the Tower it would mean change. There has to be change in order to go forward, and we must do the changing or else it will be done for us, for circumstance deals the same cards to one and all. However, attitude is the vehicle that will take us a long way toward our hopes and dreams, and -- after all -- we each are in the driver's seat.

This evening has been mixed with the mood of change and expectancy. I have also been aware of an underlying current of what the knothole has meant. It is through this small window on my world that the magic potion, out of which friendship is built, has passed. I have also learned that friendship is the glue that holds fast all the attitudes we have toward one another and enables us to prize our differences. It would be a boring world if we were all the same.

When I finally settle into the warmth and comfort of my own tick, the peace and mystery of sleep overtakes me and in the silence I will dream about the past, and be restored and renewed to live out my life at the edge of the garden, tomorrow and tomorrow and tomorrow. . . .

The Tower of Mattie Grey

After the excitement of James' wedding and the reception in the tower, I had much to consider in moving into my new home.

Tower living was much different. I had thought that to elevate my living quarters would enable me to see more and further than I ever had, but with- out the knothole, all that passed my windows was the fog and mist that hung there until the sun arose each day to burn it off. Most of my friends stopped coming when they learned I had closed the kitchen. Mr. Toad complained of the steps, and many days I met him at the foot of the stairs and he would take me out to dine at the better places.

As this routine settled over me I realized that friendship, at whatever cost, is to be valued. Mrs. Crow has taken over the gardenhouse kitchen, and I can hear the merry laughter wafting through the tower when the breeze is blowing in the right direction. I seldom joined them now, mostly because the cooking is not to my liking. I continued to think about choice and change as I settled in under my tin-topped tower, where sound was more telling than sight. I would hear noises in the night when a certain mouse family who had built in a drain pipe would be washed right out into the yard every time there was a heavy rainfall. It was a mystery why they built right back as soon as the sun came out. I would forget about this until it rained again and evidently they did also.

My dwelling and its appointments leave nothing to wish for, but as the days passed, I found myself in the garden more and more. The old chair inside the garden gate has long ago conformed to the shape of comfort, and I have felt the romance of spring in the garden and all my summers have been love affairs.

If one can imagine a perfect transparent circle rotating through the mists of time, then one may see the earth as a conservatory. The laws that govern the garden are absolute. These laws are written indelibly and locked inside a seed. We watch the great drama unfold that is reenacted on a twenty-four hour basis. So I sit in the garden both day and night.

Underneath the upper crust another world of willing workers go about their job under our feet, and many of them work the nightshift, mining the soil as they plough to aerate and condition the underground. They all have their colorful ways, and some of them fiddle and sing. There are also workers who live in the sunlight, the birds and bees who have wings to fly. I listen to their soft praise-like mutterings that will shortly change to glorious singing. I have often imagined that happiness is hidden among the beauty and music of birds.

In this setting I feel the cares of the day being lifted. The dew is on the leaf and the hour to dream has come. The flowers are like royalty dressed in velvet and silk. The monarch butterfly is crowned with moon beams and the white moth delicate as the moon light. There is the handsome toad who lives under the garden gate, and the wrinkled tissue paper blooms that serve beauty and seed to bridge the future gap. I saw the poppy smile at the thought of that.

The butterflies are served from tulip cups and bees are making flower flavored honey. One lone bee hovers over his bed time ritual and accidentally rings the foxglove bell; every one within ear shot listens until the silence is again deep and profound. I hear the whisper of gossamer wings passing over the garden gate and on to the hive. The sweet peas are beginning to climb, like toddlers, holding onto whatever is near. Roses and honeysuckle send the perfume they are wearing as far as breezes go. Daisies count their petals and ask 'Does he love me or does he not' as the satin petals are shed one by one. The night bloomers tremble as they open; they are the evening primroses and moonflowers that whisper in the dark.

The hour of twilight strikes a lower key as the shades of night deepen. Stars show up in the distance and remind me of crowns, head gear of one size that fits all. It is time to go in and the moon will light my path to the stairway leading to my bed. This night as I was preparing for bed I looked through my window and saw the night sky as my roof and the earth is surely my home. In such a setting I believe my dreams will all come true.

Since moving into the tower, I have missed the company of Mr. Toad, and every time he mentions how difficult the stairs are, I have dreamed of a way to move our relationship into a more permanent state. I know that he has never relished the idea of being tied down, but if there were some way I could dangle the good angle of all he cherishes, like my good cooking, trimming his toenails, cutting his hair, and making sure his camel-hair coat is always on right side out, he might be persuaded.

So, I planned to propose marriage the first time an opportunity arose. One thing I was sure of was Mr. Toad's undying devotion. Since he always goes home promptly at 4 o'clock in the evening, I thought it might be best to get this over with.

My strongest connection with life has been my love for the garden, so my joy will know no bounds in this setting. O spring, when all of life is sparkling and bursting out of shells, I will burst out of mine also. It really does not matter what anyone else may think. I have lived a very long time and encountered all of life's many sides. Nothing is new to me and I am able to pretend even to the point of veils and trains.

Mr. Toad likes a good show, and as the evening comes we will linger in the twilight and dream of love blooming in the garden.

A GIANT NAMED YES

Beyond the will and sight persist
A positive force does exist,
A Giant Named Yes that nothing can resist.
Beyond the scope and voice of sound
Within the deepest human realm
Thought rocks the boat, but also mans the helm
It is in giving thought to thought
From our dreams life is caught.
Yes can scale the highest wall
And do our bidding all in all.
Weeds will also grow in fertile soil,
Belief agrees to make it so.
When one thinks yes instead of no
Indecision is a thief, behold your prize
When YES becomes Belief.
Faith is feeble lacking sight,
Belief is like a shadow in the night.
The farthest out on any limb
That anyone has ever been
The absolute, right is right.
Yes is the giant whose candle gives us light.

Thank you for reading my diary. I would like to invite each of you into my world of make believe, for I believe it to be the basis of reality.   Joy Huffman

Dedications and Acknowledgments

Our lives touch one another, and we pass on, but the imprint remains. In thinking of all the impressions I have stamped upon my heart, I dedicate *The Diary of Mattie Grey* to children of all ages and the following people, who have made a contribution to my life:

> To the memory of my mother, whose first stamp of approval set the stage for my life.

> To Jim Connell, my friend, who really believes in the person of Mattie Grey.

> To Judith Caldwell Ayers, who made *The Diary of Mattie Grey* possible by all of the copy work and her belief that it is a worthwhile project.

> To Cathy Hewes Ceritano for the portrait of Mattie, which resides on my wall and is reproduced on the cover of this diary.

> To Rachael Garrity and Mary Jakubowski, my thanks and gratitude for sharing their knowledge of book matter.

> To my family, past and present, who are links in both directions.

About the Author

Joy Huffman was born June 4, 1928, and was reared in Craig County, Virginia. She graduated from New Castle High School in 1946 and from the Roanoke Memorial Hospital School of Practical Nursing in Roanoke, Virginia, in 1960.

She was married to Harold Carter Huffman. They had one son, Michael Penn. Michael Huffman and his family live in Tennessee, where he writes music.

The counties of Craig and Giles have been home to Joy Huffman all of her life, but she has seen the world through her knothole.

Made in the USA
Charleston, SC
26 October 2012